MW01097580

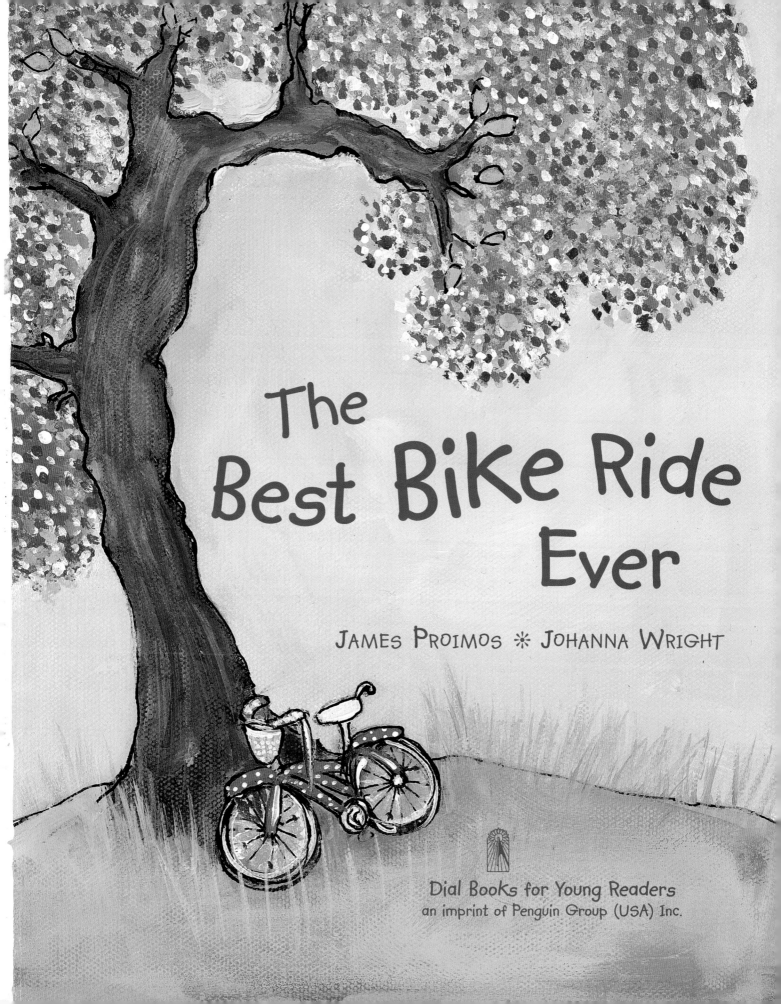

The Best Bike Ride Ever

JAMES PROIMOS ✳ JOHANNA WRIGHT

Dial Books for Young Readers
an imprint of Penguin Group (USA) Inc.

DIAL BOOKS FOR YOUNG READERS
A division of Penguin Young Readers Group
Published by The Penguin Group
Penguin Group (USA) Inc., 375 Hudson
Street, New York, NY 10014, U.S.A.
Penguin Group (Canada), 90 Eglinton Avenue
East, Suite 700, Toronto, Ontario, Canada
M4P 2Y3 (a division of Pearson Penguin Canada
Inc.) • Penguin Books Ltd, 80 Strand, London WC2R 0RL,
England • Penguin Ireland, 25 St. Stephen's Green, Dublin 2,
Ireland (a division of Penguin Books Ltd) • Penguin Group (Australia),
250 Camberwell Road, Camberwell, Victoria 3124, Australia (a division of
Pearson Australia Group Pty Ltd) • Penguin Books India Pvt Ltd, 11 Community Centre,
Panchsheel Park, New Delhi - 110 017, India • Penguin Group (NZ), 67 Apollo Drive, Rosedale,
North Shore 0632, New Zealand (a division of Pearson New Zealand Ltd) • Penguin Books (South Africa) (Pty) Ltd, 24 Sturdee Avenue,
Rosebank, Johannesburg 2196, South Africa • Penguin Books Ltd, Registered Offices: 80 Strand, London WC2R 0RL, England
Text copyright © 2012 by James Proimos • Pictures copyright © 2012 by Johanna Wright

Designed by Jennifer Kelly • Text set in Kidprint MT Std • Manufactured in China on acid-free paper
10 9 8 7 6 5 4 3 2 1
Library of Congress Cataloging-in-Publication Data available

The art was created by hand, with layers of acrylic paint on stretched canvas. The images are outlined in black India ink.

For Annie —JP

For Juniper —JW

"I want a bike!

I want a bike!

I want a bike!"

That was all Bonnie O'Boy said for one full week.

Until the eighth day, when she got a bike, which is the day she started saying "Oh boy!

Thank you, Mother! Thank you, Father!"

"Thank you, Charley!"

Bang Bang
Bang

Although her brother, Charley, was busy building this and that and had nothing to do with her getting a bike.

Now Bonnie O'Boy also had a question.

"May I go ride my bike?"

"Well, before you go, you have to know how to stop—"

"You can't just go ride all willy-nilly—"

But it was too late.

Bonnie O'Boy had already gone all willy-nilly.
In fact, she had willy-nillied herself right down the hill.

"Wait! Stop!"

And so Bonnie O'Boy rode her bike.

She rode her bike over bridges.

Over mountains.

Over elephants.

But she could not stop.

She rode her bike through downpours.

Through windstorms.

She rode her bike to the **top** of the Statue of Liberty.

Down
to the
bottom
of the

Grand
Canyon.

Past the Giant Cheese . . .

. . . and into the
Land of the Lost.

But as much as she tried,
Bonnie O'Boy could not stop.

Not stopping was thrilling.

Not stopping was breathtaking.

Not stopping was dangerous.

Not stopping was—

Oof!

Bonnie had stopped.

Scraped knee and all.

Her mother, who had been close behind, put a Band-Aid on the boo-boo and said "I love you" instead of "I told you so."

Her father hugged her tight and gave her a proper bike lesson.

"Here are the brakes."

Her brother, Charley . . . well, he was already back to work.

And so for one full week, Bonnie O'Boy didn't say a word.
She just rode her bike, stopping often to smell the roses . . .

and making secret wishes
she was not ready to tell anyone.